MONSTERS
Pick Your Path

Secret Stowaway

4

SUNBIRD
PENGUIN

Published by Ladybird Books Ltd 2012

A Penguin Company
Penguin Books Ltd, 80 Strand, London, WC2R 0RL, UK
Penguin Group (USA) Inc., 375 Hudson Street, New York 10014, USA
Penguin Books Australia Ltd, Camberwell Road, Camberwell, Victoria 3124,
Australia (A division of Pearson Australia Group Pty Ltd)
Penguin Group (NZ), 67 Apollo Drive, Rosedale, Auckland 0632,
New Zealand (a division of Pearson New Zealand Ltd)
Canada, India, South Africa

Sunbird is a trade mark of Ladybird Books Ltd

© Mind Candy Ltd. Moshi Monsters is a trademark
of Mind Candy Ltd. All rights reserved.

By Ian Pike

www.ladybird.com

ISBN: 978-1-40939 - 091 - 6

002

Printed in Great Britain

MIX
Paper from
responsible sources
FSC   FSC® C018179

To claim your exclusive virtual gift,
go to the sign-in page of

MOSHIMONSTERS.COM

And enter the eighth word on the seventh
line of the thirteenth page of this book!
Your surprise free gift will appear
in your treasure chest!

You peer out from behind your hiding place.
There she is, Bushy Fandango. Explorer extraordinaire. Scared of nothing. So intrepid that when she isn't exploring, she takes holidays in the sub-zero temperatures of the Yappalation Mountains. Her team of trusty White Fang Musky Huskies always by her side, she can be spotted exploring the snowy wilds, seeking out adventure and treasures to bring back to the Bizarre Bazaar. The Musky Huskies are clearly chomping at the bit right now, ready for the off and you are desperate to go with her but you also know that she would definitely say no if you asked.

You give it a great deal of thought but in the end decide, there's only one thing for it; you have to stowaway. You have been desperate to join her for so long and now feels like it might be your last chance. You do hesitate for just a second, thinking of the dangers but soon dismiss them. You would surely regret it forever.

But which of her expeditions should you join her on? The talk all over Monstro City is that she's planning on some of the most daring journeys ever attempted. You feel a shiver of fear run up and down your spine. Once you are hidden away, there can be no change of heart. You almost abandon the plan there and then. There's no getting away from the fact that this could be scary. However, you steel yourself and move into position on the back of her old mountain wagon.

But where are you going? Bushy has been boasting of journeys into some of the darkest corners of the world of Moshi for some time now, and here you are stepping out into the unknown.

To hide away on Bushy's trip to Mount Sillimanjaro as she seeks out a rare boil 'n' bubble cauldron, **turn to page 21.**

To stowaway on an underwater adventure with Bushy heading down to the bottom of Potion Ocean to hunt for the famous Black Pearl, **turn to page 23.**

To head to the volcanic island of Emberooze to assist Bushy in tracking down some exotic worm earrings, **go to page 13.**

To secretly join her on a dangerous mission into the depths of the Gombala Gombala Jungle in search of an 18 Carat Parrot, **turn to page 78.**

Or, to stay closer to home and hideaway on her assignment to Flutterby Field in search of rare flutterbies to bring back to the Bizarre Bazaar, **turn to page 57.**

You are completely out of breath. You decided to chase after Bushy's wagon but the Huskies are keeping up quite a speed. However, you are gaining on them.

'Bushy!' you shout. 'Just turn around, please.'

But she still hears nothing. Then disaster strikes. Well, it could have happened to anyone. You were hot on the trail of Bushy and her wagon. Just rounding the corner, seconds away from being able to catch up with them completely and then BAM! Foolishly, you managed to unleash a ClothEared Cloud Formation having accidentally shouted 'Woo-oo-oo!' while trying to attract Bushy. Already things are starting to get very spooky.

For starters, you are now trapped in a parallel vortex inhabited only by Fancy Banshees – and they have you completely surrounded. The Banshees are supernatural Spookie Moshlings. They can be a little creepy but most of them are pretty friendly. However, you are starting to get just the tiniest bit nervous as they float just that little bit closer to you than you would like.

'Come on guys, this isn't funny,' you object, doing your best to appeal to their better nature. You know that one touch of their shimmering capes could turn you inside out in a flash!

'How about we make a little deal?' you ask. 'There must be something we can trade for my freedom?'

The Banshees 'um' and 'ah' for a bit, but it turns out they do need something. Luckily, it's something you can help with. They are in desperate need of a fresh supply of Rox dust and you just so happened to spot some earlier, floating about in the atmosphere above the spot where you fell before. You are happy to lead them there, as long as they let you continue on your way. The only trouble is, once you've showed them where to collect the dust and restore their fading glow, you realise that you now have no hope of catching Bushy.

But just then, with a whoosh and a whirr, Roy G. Biv whizzes past on a rainbow! Fantastic! He only comes by once a year to make sure we have rainbows all year round.

You have two choices.

You can try and pick up the trail once again, and hope against all hope that you manage to locate Bushy. To do this, **turn to page 11.**

Or, you could attempt to attract Roy G. Biv's attention to see if he can help. In which case, **turn to page 20.**

'Right,' you say, tuning up. 'Now, it's been a while since I last strummed the old five string, but I should be able to give it some sort of a go.'

Da, da, lang, lang, lang, dang, dang, you pluck, as Bushy winces.

'Hang on a minute; I'll remember how to play in a second.'

'Don't worry about the tune. Just try making it as loud as you possibly can. We need to wake him if possible, not serenade the old thing,' she says.

Da, da, lang, lang, lang, dang, daaaaaannnggggg!!!!!! You play with all your might.

The Snoring Hickopotumus slowly opens an eye.

'You'd better have another go,' asks Bushy. 'Even louder this time.'

So you give it all you've got. You might be strumming a banjo here but in your head you're in front of a crowd of thousands of screaming fans in Trembly Stadium.

The Hickopotumus' other eye opens and he lets out a great yawn.

'And again please,' yells Bushy. 'Fill your boots.'

Your fingers are in agony as you pluck away and you wonder just how much you've got left in you, but then the Hickopotumus lumbers to his feet and shuffles off the path.

The music might be enough to wake him, but that doesn't necessarily mean he's enjoying the way you're playing it.

'Quick,' yells Bushy. 'Now's our chance'

Before you get a chance to proceed however, the

Hickopotamus plucks the banjo from your grasp. He yawns widely, settles back down in the middle of the road, then begins picking away on the banjo. He's far more tuneful than you were and you're mesmerized by his playing. You sit down, hoping to pick up some tips. Bushy sighs and sits down too. Clearly you're not going anywhere any time soon . . .

THE END

You decide to try and follow your nose, hoping that somehow this will eventually lead you to where Bushy is currently searching for an 18 Carat Shiny Parrot. Sadly, you're just heading deeper and deeper into the jungle. You are completely lost and not afraid to admit it. The more you try and find a way out of the jungle, the more lost you seem to be getting. This really is serious and unfortunately things get even worse.

'Ow!' you shriek, feeling a scratch. 'That can't be good.'

It isn't. You look down and see a rash beginning to spread. A feeling of faintness is quickly washing over you. You stagger a little before slumping to your knees, noticing as you go down that a strange green and pink, spiky plant is by your side. You must have brushed past it. Judging from the way you are feeling, it must be poisonous. You collapse in a heap on the floor. The last thing you remember is seeing a woolly blue creature looming over you, clutching a pink staff with a skull on the top.

Once you've come round, you find the Moshling tending to your wounds. He is rubbing on a potion made of exotic leaves, and you realise that it must be Big Bad Bill, the Woolly Blue Hoodoo. They are wise old Moshlings who know everything there is to know about lotions, potions and spells. He may very well have saved your life, but before you have time to thank him, the sound of yapping sends him scurrying off back into the jungle and you find yourself surrounded by Musky Huskies. As you look up, you see Bushy standing over you, clutching a shiny bird of some sort. She must have completed her quest and then stumbled across you on the way back.

'Boy, are you a sight for sore eyes,' you say, as she lifts you onto the wagon. You are safe once more – and most definitely ready to head home.

THE END

You can't stop smiling. Here you are on an actual Bushy Fandango expedition and she even seems pleased to have you on board! As you stand on the deck of her boat, you realise that this is all a dream come true. But then, out of the blue, a hammer blow comes crashing down and shatters your dreams into a million pieces.

'On second thoughts, you can't go to Emberooze,' sighs Bushy. 'Sorry, but it just won't be possible now.'

You can hardly believe it. To get as close as to be actually helping to load up the boat, only to then have to turn back would be almost heartbreaking. Especially as Bushy had been talking through her plans to hunt down and bring back some exotic worm earrings. They are as rare as they are tricky to capture, but you really fancied having a go.

'But why?' you ask. 'I've come all this way now.'

Bushy shakes her head sadly. 'Emberooze is a volcanic island and reports from *The Daily Growl* suggest it's about to erupt. It's far too dangerous.'

'But you're still going there,' you plead.

'That's a risk I can take. No way can I place an amateur in such danger.'

You shake your head, annoyed.

'I can do it, Bushy. Please?'

Bushy looks you over for a second. 'Of course, I can't physically stop you from coming, but it could be treacherous. Besides, I have a different job for you, if you're interested.'

You stare back at her hopefully.

'There is another way to track down an exotic worm earring,' she continues. 'You see, they can also be found deep within the Barmy Swami Jungle. If you were to head there for me, I'd be most grateful.'

You stare at her, torn. Both sound like awesome adventures.

'There's no guarantee I'll be able to make it to Emberooze anyway,' she says, 'so it would be great to have a backup plan.'

You think hard. It's tempting, as there's always the possibility that she'll have to turn back from Emberooze anyway.

'One more thing before you make a final decision,' adds Bushy. 'You'd have to find a way to infiltrate the Snuggly Tiger Cubs in the jungle. Snuggly Tiger Cubs, in particular, are very protective of the exotic worms.'

What to do? To head for the Barmy Swami Jungle, **turn to page 30.**

Or, to continue on to Emberooze Island with Bushy, **turn to page 42.**

As you make your way round the outskirts of the field, you start thinking that maybe this could be even harder than you first thought. I mean, how do you startle a flutterby? Can you just leap out and make a loud noise? But then what if it doesn't scare easily? Some creatures don't. And what if you do manage to startle it, but it just flaps off in a completely different direction? Then what would Bushy say? Questions, questions, questions.

You stop and watch the flutterby darting hither and occasionally thither between flowers, and are struck once again by just how colourful it actually is. It really is a thing of beauty, and it almost seems a shame to catch it. Then again, at least you know it will be well looked after back at the Bizarre Bazaar.

You shuffle forward and get as close as you can without letting the flutterby know you are there. When you think you are as near as can be without giving away your hiding place, you stop and think for a second. You need complete silence until you spring out and rush towards the flutterby, as you have to make absolutely sure that it flies straight across to Bushy. Sadly however, total silence is suddenly lacking around here. Some kind of singing seems to be coming from the middle of the next field and there is a right old clamour coming from the sky above. You creep back a pace or two and survey the scene. Luckily, the flutterby hasn't been frightened off yet.

The singing is coming from a picnicking couple nearby. Lila Tweet and her friend Pete Slurp are contentedly munching away on some Roarberry Cheesecake as they sit back on a blanket. In between mouthfuls, Lila sings away happily like a little songbird. Lila is famous for her singing but her best friend Pete is tone deaf. He is however amazing at collecting rare slugs

Then, as you look upwards, you spot Chick Checker passing overhead making his usual racket. Two lots of noise from two separate directions! As you take in the din, you are struck by an idea. Chick, Lila and Pete could help you get the flutterby back to Bushy.

To use Lila Tweet's singing to try and lull the flutterby over, **turn to page 71.**

Or, to use Chick Checker's cacophony to scare the flutterby back to Bushy, **turn to page 25.**

You decide to organise a barn dance to try and rouse the Snoring Hickopotumus. The music is really pumping and Bushy is doing her best to call a line dance. Not the easiest thing in the world when there's only you and a load of Musky Huskies to join in.

'Right, come on you lot, it's simple. Take your partner by the paw and . . . '

She stops. Two of the Musky Huskies have come to a standstill and are just howling along to the music. But the Hickopotumus is still snoring. Bushy starts to become a little impatient.

'Can we all please concentrate? If we don't shift him soon, we won't stand a chance of finding that exotic worm. Now, please. Do-si-do on my count. One, two, three . . . '

And you're off. Forwards, backwards, round the side. Step and hop and clap and back. Sadly, none of it is working. The Hickopotumus is still snoring away.

'We're really going to have to go bananas if this is going to stand any chance of working. Crack that whip, Huskies. Dance like you've never danced before.'

Before you know it, you are really giving it some. You always knew that a barn dance could be fun, but this is fangtastic. It's the best fun ever! But still, the Hickopotumus sleeps on. Bushy stops calling out the moves... and sighs deeply.

'This is never going to work,' she cries. 'Honestly, how can anything sleep so much?'

Then, you have a brainwave.

'Hicko firewater!' you shout.

'Bless you,' says Bushy.

'No. I mean, we need some to wake him. A drop of that stuff should do the job.'

Bushy soon manages to dig some out of her expedition supplies. However, wafting it under the Hickopotumus' nose has no effect. You, Bushy and the Huskies might all have tears in your eyes from the pong, but on he snores. Luckily, you have a backup plan.

'Enchanted corn,' you cry.

'Will you please stop doing that?' asks a startled Bushy. 'Nearly jumped out of my fur.'

'Sorry, but we need to cook some up. If the smell of that doesn't wake him, nothing will.'

Unfortunately, it doesn't seem to be working. But you're not one for quitting easily.

'Bung in three parts Hot Silly Peppers, two parts Magic Beans, and then add in just the lightest dusting of Crazy Daisies,' you yell, bossing the Huskies and Bushy around. It takes a bit of hunting for the rest of the ingredients, but soon enough there is a pungent smell wafting about.

'A few more Hot Silly Peppers!' you shout. 'Now, fan that smoke towards him. That's it.' You are building up quite a sweat as you direct the others with their work, but this must work. You really have tried everything else to shift the Hickopotumus and nothing has even begun to make him stir.

Then, he sits up abruptly. Bolt upright and wide awake. And taking you all completely by surprise, he's suddenly up and jigging away along to the barn dance music.

You turn to look at Bushy. 'That's not quite what I was expecting.'

Bushy shrugs. 'Well, it definitely worked. Look at him go.'

You both watch for a second.

'I suppose we should head off and find that exotic worm earring now,' Bushy says.

You turn and smile as the Huskies join in with the Hickopotumus in a totally bonkers line dance. 'No particular rush is there? Not now everyone's having so much fun.'

You grab hold of Bushy and the Hickopotumus and step into the line. You've waited long enough to secure the latest addition to Bushy's collection – a few more hours won't matter.

THE END

This was definitely a wise thing to do. Roy G. Biv is just such a dude and asking him for help was the best idea ever. He's the greatest Sky Surfer there is, the most rad Rainbow Rider, and a Cloud Cruiser like no other. Without exaggeration, Roy G. Biv rocks, and here you are on a rainbow-riding mission with him! You are not just helping him make sure that there are rainbows all year round in Monstro City; you are also hoping to spot Bushy from up above while you whirl about in the air.

'**Wheeeeeee!**' you shout, giddy with excitement as Roy hangs a sharp turn and you skim over the indigo stripe of the rainbow.

'**Wwwwwwwwwoooooooaahhhh!**' you yell, as he whooshes quickly over the yellow stripe.

'**This is aaaammmmaaaazzziiinggg!**' you cry.

At least it would be, were it not for the fact that the next really sharp turn makes you lose your balance slightly. You are thrown off balance and find yourself clinging on for dear life to the edge of the Colossal Cloud Cruiser, feeling yourself slipping by the second . . .

You look down and realise that you have two choices.

You can either drop safely into The Port, by **turning to page 32.**

Or, you could always try and land on a Plasma Cloud. It's certainly riskier, but at least you won't get so wet. If you think this is the best thing to do, **turn to page 28.**

You decide to hide away as Bushy heads off to Mount Sillimanjaro in search of a rare boil 'n' bubble cauldron, but are now wondering if it really was the best idea ever. You clambered on board Bushy's exploration wagon while nobody was looking and were very nearly sniffed out by one of the Huskies. You are stuck between two boxes with a sharp corner digging into you, and you're just about to give yourself up, when you hear a sudden noise.

'**Owwwww!**' Bushy cries out, sounding like she is pain. '**Oooooowwwwwwwwwwaaahhh!**'

She is definitely hurt, and you are very much aware that there's nobody else around but you who can help her. Well, unless you count the slightly whiffy Huskies who are now making more noise than ever.

Quietly, you creep out from your poky hiding place. You are pleased to be free, but worried at what might happen now that your secret is out. Bushy is lying down clutching her leg, with her foot clearly trapped under her wagon. You cough quietly to let her know that you are there. She stops shrieking for a second and stares.

'What the . . . who? I mean, where the what? Why? How? And hey!'

'I'm really sorry, Bushy. I just wanted to go on your expedition so badly and I knew that if I asked you'd say no, so I hid away, but then I heard you were in pain, and . . . '

Bushy holds up a hand.

'Please. Is there any chance you could help get me out of here first? Then you can tell me everything. I am just slightly worried that my leg might fall off.'

'Oh . . . yes,' you reply.

You can also see that her foot is starting to turn blue. Even though it now matches her hair, it's clearly not a good thing.

You heave at the wagon with all your might and just about manage to lift it high enough for her to escape. As you check her over, you realise that although she might be free, there's no way she can go anywhere. Not with her foot looking like that.

'Botheration!' she exclaims. 'That was my one chance to track down a boil 'n' bubble cauldron.'

The Huskies are almost frantic with excitement and frustration, as is Bushy. She looks at the Huskies, then at her foot. Then finally, she looks at you.

'I don't suppose you'd . . . ? I mean . . . no. It would be too much to ask.'

Could it really be? Is the great explorer herself actually asking you to take on an expedition on your own? But then what would happen to Bushy? You couldn't just leave her here alone . . . Or could you? She must have been in worse situations.

To take Bushy back to Monstro City, **turn to page 26.**

Or, to continue on the adventure to Mount Sillimanjaro, **turn to page 36.**

There is great excitement in Monstro City. Bushy Fandango's announcement that she is planning an underwater expedition to the bottom of Potion Ocean has sent ripples throughout the land. And here you are, uninvited, hiding out in her specially crafted Fandango sub as it hurtles down towards the bottom of the sea. You managed to sneak in by stowing away in the diving equipment. You decide that you had better face the music sooner rather than later, so creep out from your hiding place and cough loudly to let Bushy know you are there.

She stares at you in stunned silence for a second or two.

'I really must be dreaming. A stowaway? Do you have any idea how dangerous this could be? Bushy asks, clearly very concerned.

You start to explain how you knew that it was wrong, but you were so desperate to join her on an adventure and knew that she would have said no if you had asked her. However, something stops you. An almighty crash and a huge thud ricochet round the sub as if something has just struck the side of the vessel. Bushy is thrown off her feet, and through the panicked pandemonium of the yelping Huskies you rush to look out of a porthole. You can hardly believe your eyes.

'What is it?' calls Bushy, clambering to her feet and dusting herself off.

'It would seem that Captain Buck E. Barnacle is attempting to capture your sub,' you call back. 'Looks to me like he's gone totally bonkers.'

Bushy joins you quickly, as another crash rings out from above.

'You're right,' says Bushy. 'I'd never believe such a thing were possible if I wasn't seeing it with my own eyes.'

'Why would Cap'n Buck want to catch you?' you wonder. 'That's not like him.'

'Not unless he's been turned somehow,' suggests Bushy, watching as he launches yet another assault. He is currently hurling seaweed bombs at you from the Cloudy Cloth Clipper's underwater exploration pod.

'You don't mean . . . ?' You can hardly dare to say it.

'Fraid so. I smell the wicked glove of Dr. Strangelove – and I don't mean like that time when he'd been juggling with mouldy Mutant Sprouts.'

You are busy wondering to yourself how such a gentle monster as the Captain could be under Strangeglove's spell, when Bushy snaps you out of it.

'Come on. We need to do something about this now or it'll be curtains for us all. And I don't mean the nice rose-tinted ones for heart-shaped windows. One of us needs to provide a distraction while the other stays here and tries to hold him back. At least until the spell wears off.'

To be the one to provide the distraction, **turn to page 34.**

Or, to stay and fend off Cap'n Buck, **turn to page 56.**

You thought that Chick Checker might be able to help. His noisy 'peeps' are legendary throughout the whole of Monstro City, and there isn't a single Monster or Moshling that hasn't been kept awake at night by him at some point. In this instance he was on his way back to Gift Island when you heard him, but luckily you still managed to attract his attention. It wasn't easy over the din he was making, but you were able to hail him down and are now busy explaining the situation. You do your best to get him to help. Luckily, you still manage to get him to understand your needs.

'Right, all you have to do is give it as much volume as possible. 'Loud as you can,' you explain. 'Then hopefully, the flutterby should be spooked into flapping away and I'll do my best to steer it towards Bushy.'

You ask him to give you a minute, before rushing back to stand just out of reach of the flutterby. When Bushy is ready, you give the signal and Chick opens up his lungs. He gives it his all, and it really is some noise. As soon as the flutterby hears the din, it sets off into the air.

Then, thanks to you rushing towards it, it soon finds itself heading towards Bushy's waiting net. Between the three of you, you've managed the capture and are finally able to head home. Mission accomplished!

What's even more exciting is that word is out on your exciting find and Roary Scrawl is desperate to write a column on the rare flutterby and your part in tracking it down in The Daily Growl. Fame at last!

THE END

'How on earth did you manage to talk me into this?' Bushy asks.

She has been looking worried ever since you slung her onto the wagon and started heaving her back to Monstro City. 'Think of all the excitement we're missing out on.'

'Can you please keep still for a second?' you say. 'We need to get you seen to.'

'I'll be fine,' whimpers Bushy sadly. 'I have been stranded in far worse conditions with nothing to live off but spider lollies and sour milk, you know.'

You sigh deeply. This could be a long journey home. But just as you reach Monstro City, something makes you stop short. An excited mob seems to be waiting for the arrival of something, or indeed someone. It's only when Roary Scrawl and Ruby Scribblez burst through the crowd and run towards you, that you realise it's you they've gathered to see. You seem to have become a celebrity.

Roary is after all the editor in chief of the Daily Growl. While Ruby, self-made expert on all things Moshi, looks after *Shrillboard Magazine* and does a regular blog for Roary. They don't come out for just anyone.

'Is it true you stowed away?'

'Can you confirm that you single-handedly rescued Bushy Fandango?'

Ruby and Roary are both firing questions at you, but you have to make sure that Bushy is properly looked after before talking to them.

'Would you give us an exclusive interview?' Ruby persists, refusing to give up.

As Bushy hauls herself up onto her good foot, you realise that she is going to be okay. Besides, everyone is now clambering over to help her. Ruby looks at you.

'Please talk to us. Everyone's desperate to hear your story and you really are a hero.'

Bushy nods. 'Go on then, superstar. After all, you did rescue me.'

You smile and head off towards the Moshi TV studio. You might not have made it on one of Bushy's expeditions, but this new life as a celebrity could definitely help you to forget what might have been!

THE END

After deciding that the best option is to drop off the Colossal Cloud Cruiser and land in a Plasma Cloud, you now find yourself hurtling downwards faster than a Disco Duckie to a dancefloor. The soft, fluffy, cotton-like cloud safely cushions your landing.

You waft some cloud out of your eyes and peer around. You'd been wondering, as you fell, what to do once you landed in here. It was only ever going to be one step on the way down and if you're honest, there's still a lot more air below you to fall through. What you hadn't expected to find was that the cloud was already inhabited, as you can now tell due to the fact that a small pair of smiling eyes are looking back at you.

It's Kissy the Baby Ghost. You'd recognise her anywhere. This Spookie might be shy, but she's currently flapping her huge eyelashes at you very cutely. Well, she is a supernatural Moshling more interested in toys, tutus and false eyelashes than being scary.

'Hello,' you say. 'Sorry for dropping in like this. Bit of an emergency.' You peer down at the huge gap below, wondering if you will now be doomed to spend the rest of your days in this cloud, or at least stuck here until it evaporates. If so, goodness knows what might happen.

Luckily, Kissy has a solution. She offers to lend you her pink, fluffy blanket to use as a parachute, as long as you don't mind telling her favourite story first. You do your best to remember Ghouldilocks and the Three Scares, which you just about manage. Once you've reached the end, she hands over her blanket and you find yourself plummeting downwards once more.

As you hurtle towards The Port, you spot Bushy and the Musky Huskies in the distance.

You can either continue to drop into The Port, by **turning to page 32.**

Or, you could try and divert your fall towards Bushy to finish off the quest for the 18 Carat Shiny Parrot, by **turning to page 65.**

You very sensibly decide not to continue with the risky journey to Emberooze, so are now beating a path through the tropical forestry of the Barmy Swami Jungle instead. It is swelteringly hot and sticky and mysterious things keep trying to nibble on you, but you couldn't be happier. You have been entrusted with a mission from Bushy and you love the responsibility. This is what it's all about – exploration and adventure! Suddenly, you hear a noise. You stop. Hidden away in the lush foliage of the jungle, you spot a flash of yellow and black stripes. It's Jeepers the Snuggly Tiger Cub. An adorable Moshling who really has earned his stripes. That's because the Jeepers spend ages painting them on using inka-inka juice, squeezed from rare thumpkin seeds. Sadly the jungle is green, not yellow and stripy.

He's sitting down, munching away on some Red Crazy Daisy leaves and shoots. Every now and then, he stops and purrs contentedly. He really is adorable. Then you notice something sparkling in the ground. It's a creature of some sort, but one that glistens like gold and is like nothing you have ever seen before. It looks a bit like a wiggly worm covered in diamonds.

'Wow,' you whisper, edging forward to get a closer look. This is so far out of the ordinary. It's part jewel, part creature and there are several of them burrowing about in front of you. These must be the famous exotic worms that Bushy wants you to find. But how are you going to get one without Jeepers noticing?

The answer is staring you in the face. Well, Jeepers

is at least. Your 'wow' must have been louder than you thought. You step forward but Jeepers immediately moves out of the foliage, protecting his territory. This is going to be harder than you thought.

'Think, think, think,' you mutter to yourself, desperately wracking your brains for an answer. 'What can you remember about Snuggly Tiger Cubs?' And then it hits you.

'Ow!' you shout. You must have walked into a branch.

Luckily, the bump to your head helps you remember something Buster once told you about Jeepers. He loves glam rock and you just so happen to have a music player and a few kicking tracks lined up in your backpack. Seconds later, you're playing a groovy tune and he is edging even further towards you.

'That's it. You'll enjoy this one . . . listen,' you coax.

Before you know it, he's strutting around the forest.

Moments later, you are able to slip past him with a number of very wriggly exotic worms in your hand to take back to Bushy. She'll be over the moon with your efforts!

THE END

As you hurtle down towards The Port, you realise just how fast you are actually travelling. Maybe you haven't thought this through properly. Wow! That water sure is approaching fast. You brace yourself for impact and in you go . . . **sssppplllaaaassshhh!**

Oooohhhhwww, that's cold you think, shivering as you swim back up to the surface. You take in your surroundings. You really are in the middle of The Port with nothing to do but bob about and hope to be rescued or try and swim to the shore. Before you even have time to think about how that might actually happen, you feel yourself being pulled towards the shore.

'Woah! Where am I going now?' you call out, though there seems to be no one around to call out to. Then suddenly, you spot him. Heaving away, rod in hand and almost unable to believe he has finally caught something, is Billy Bob Baitman. He's famous for never catching anything and yet here he is, pulling on what must feel to him like the catch of the season. That's when you notice the line between the end of his rod and yourself, as you spin madly towards the harbour side. Oh well, at least it's getting you out of the danger zone and giving Billy Bob a brief moment of joy. So far, the biggest thing he's caught has been an old boot!

As you reach the shore, you know that Billy Bob will be really disappointed when he realizes you are anything but a fish. Still, maybe being a hero for rescuing you will make him feel better. And at least you're finally safe and heading for home!

THE END

You decide to be the decoy to try and distract Cap'n Buck. As you launch the sub's pod, you feel a thrill of excitement. This was exactly the kind of thing you stowed away for. It's time for action!

'Oi! Landlubber!' you shout, hoping to wind him up and steer him away from the submarine.

He has clearly spotted you, as he turns his own underwater craft in your direction and gives chase. This is almost definitely down to Strangeglove or one of his C.L.O.N.C. companions. You can see that the Captain is in some sort of a trance and far from being himself, but you can't let that worry you right now. You have to get him as far away from Bushy's sub as possible until the spell wears off.

'Uh oh!' you murmur, as you spot what is up ahead. It's a great underwater rock formation and there is literally no way around it. The Captain's gaining on you. This could be it. Maybe Bushy was right; you just hadn't thought it all through when you decided to be a stowaway. It really can be dangerous. And now if you don't make it back, poor old Cap'n Buck will feel responsible forever, even though he's only behaving like a proper pirate because C.L.O.N.C. have got their claws into him. What will happen to Bushy and the Musky Huskies if you don't pull this off?

But suddenly, help is at hand. Blurp the Batty Bubblefish appears out of nowhere and unleashes an almighty splurt of multi-coloured gloop, all over poor Cap'n Buck's craft.

'Way to go, Blurp!' you cry. You are able to take full

advantage of the temporarily blind Captain and make a break for it in the pod. 'Time to get out of here!'

You quickly weave in and out of the now colourful and sticky seawater, while Blurp blows raspberries to clear a path through the foam. This creates even more bubbles, but with a little bit of luck you manage to find your way through.

As you steer the pod back to the sub, you realise it won't be long until Cap'n Buck gets bored of looking for you and goes back to his original target. The sub. You'd better get ready to defend it with Bushy. However, Blurp seems sad.

'What's up, little fish?' you ask. After all, if it wasn't for the little swimmer, you really could have been facing a very sticky end. It turns out that Blurp has a terrible problem to deal with. The trouble is, thanks to its tiny memory, it just can't remember what it actually is. All Blurp knows is that something awful happened back home at Fruit Falls. Now you have a real dilemma.

Do you head back to the sub and help Bushy fend off Cap'n Buck? If so, **turn to page 56.**

Or, if you think one good turn deserves another and want to take Blurp back to Fruit Falls, then **turn to page 38.**

Of course, you made sure Bushy was safe first. You lit a fire and checked that there was plenty of food and water at hand, with a distress flare in reach to attract rescuers. Besides, the Musky Huskies will look after her. You are now on a solo mission to complete the task, which is to find and bring back a rare boil 'n' bubble cauldron.

However, you can see that this will be far from easy. Mount Sillimanjaro is bleak and appears to be uninhabited. At least you thought it was, until you spot the signs of a base camp up ahead. And even more surprisingly, a familiar face is peering out of a tent at you.

'Buster? What are you doing here?' you cry out.

Buster Bumblechops, Monstro City's very own Moshling collector extraordinaire, is in front of you.

'Trekking holiday,' he replies, squinting at you over the top of his enormous moustache. 'What about you?'

You recount your tale of stowing away and having to rescue Bushy. You are about to explain how you've taken her place on the expedition, when Buster stops you.

'Ssshhh! Think I've just spotted one.'

You look around, confused. Spotted what?

'Tomba, a Wistful Snowtot. Been tracking the chilly chappy for days, now.'

You follow his gaze excitedly. You've always wanted to see a Snowtot and this could be your chance. Buster picks up on your excitement.

'Don't suppose you'd fancy joining me, would you? It used to be so much fun when my sidekick Snuffy came on these trips with me.'

You feel torn. Yet another dream could come true right here and now, but then again you really should complete the mission for Bushy. To top it all off, it's starting to snow.

To join Buster in seeking out Tomba, **turn to page 44.**

Or, to carry on looking for the boil 'n' bubble cauldron for Bushy, **go to page 40.**

You decide to help Blurp. Deep down, you know it's the right thing to do. Despite looking so sad and distraught, it cannot seem to remember what it is that's upsetting it. Besides, if it wasn't for the little Bubblefish, goodness knows what might have happened to you at the hands of the entranced Cap'n Buck.

As you reach Fruit Falls, you can feel Blurp beginning to tense up. You can see the other Bubblefish in the river below the Falls and clearly all is not well. Soon afterwards, you discover what the problem is. Fruit Falls is no longer flowing and neither is the river. The effect is totally batty; the Bubblefish are clearly struggling without anywhere to swim. As soon as Blurp sees the problem, it becomes even sadder. It's obvious that Blurp remembers exactly what was upsetting it, but then promptly forgets again. This cycle continues for some time. The trouble is, the Bubblefish keep spurting out gallons of gloop and it's blocking up the falls. No wonder they need your help.

'Well, it's not going to be easy but there is a way to sort this out,' you tell Blurp. 'Somehow, we're going to have to dam up the river and shift the obstruction to allow the Falls to flow once again. Then we need to provide some proper drainage for all this gloop.'

But what can you possibly get your hands on at such short notice that would provide the necessary building materials to dam up an entire gloop-filled waterfall? Your eyes scour the horizon. And then it hits you – right in the face.

'Blurp!' you cry out, wiping gunk from your eye. 'This

isn't the time to be glooping me.'

Blurp looks very apologetic but then immediately forgets why. Luckily, you spotted something before the multicoloured mess caught you in the mush.

'Old flip-flops, of course. Batty Bubblefish collect them and we're completely surrounded by the things. That's what we'll use to dam up the river.'

It's all a bit of a nightmare, but eventually you do manage to get the job done. The Bubblefish are sent off to collect the old, flippy-flappy footwear but then quickly forget what they are doing, to say nothing of the constant gloop attacking you have to put up with! Finally however, the dam is in place and you are able to head back to the sub. Now, you are fully prepared to help Bushy overcome Cap'n Buck and continue onwards to track down the Black Pearl.

To rejoin Bushy, **turn to page 56.**

You decide that your priority is to complete the task set by Bushy and go in search of an epic adventure. As you venture north in the direction suggested by Bushy, you are faced with a vast expanse of rock and little else. You seem to have ended up in the depths of the Crazy Canyons and Bushy's map is really not helping.

'Maybe being an intrepid explorer isn't all it's made out to be,' you mutter to yourself. You try to look at the map the other way round in case it helps. It doesn't, but it does look a little like a Furi at this angle.

Then you spy a spooky red glow in the distance. The closer you get, the hotter the air seems to be around the glow. Whatever it is up ahead, it's smoking hot . . . You've done it! You've found the boil 'n' bubble cauldron. As you get closer, you start to see what all the fuss is about.

'Hiccuping Hoodoos,' you whisper in awe. Hesitantly, you reach out to touch it.

'Owww!' you shout, feeling the burn creep right through your finger and up into your hand.

Getting it back to Bushy really isn't going to be easy. It's big, hot and heavy. You whistle for the Huskies and soon hear them scampering towards you. You get them to help haul Bushy's wagon over and then look round for something to help you lift this rare and exotic artefact on board. A couple of dead tree branches are near at hand and you work up quite a sweat dragging them across to the cauldron. With a lot of heaving and a smidge of hoeing, you somehow manage to jam them underneath and get it onto the wagon.

You eventually return to the spot where you left Bushy. She's clearly in a very bad mood. She is never one to enjoy sitting still at the best of times, and is no doubt feeling a bit frustrated at not being able to complete the mission herself. However, her eyes light up when she sees what you have brought back with you.

'You've really done it, haven't you?' she whispers in awe, gently reaching out towards the cauldron. 'And there was me doubting you'd ever be able to pull this off.'

You smile modestly, as she hauls herself up onto her good foot.

'The question is, my monstrous pal, where next?' she asks.

'Well, don't you want to go home? Get your leg looked at?' you answer.

'That's always a possibility, of course. But that would be boring. Dullsville. Especially when I've got another expedition planned and could really do with some help on it,' she says, with a twinkle in her eye.

You're torn. A huge part of you wants to go with her, but then again you do feel like the sensible thing would be to get her back to Monstro City.

'Come on,' she urges. 'You've clearly got what it takes and my foot feels better now, honestly.'

To accompany Bushy on another adventure, **turn to page 13.**

Or, to do the sensible thing and escort her back to Monstro City, **turn to page 26.**

41

You're a little nervous and don't mind admitting it. As you bob forward towards Emberooze Island you can feel the heat building. The volcano must have erupted already because things are definitely hotting up. As the boat crunches gently onto the pebbles beneath the lapping shore, Bushy leaps out with her Musky Huskies, excited to begin the exploration. But at that very moment, there comes an almighty roar.

'She's going to blow again!' shouts Bushy. 'I knew I should have left you behind! How on earth did you manage to talk me into it?'

With that, she grabs your hand and drags you towards the shelter of some rocks.

'No way are we going to be able to get through it,' she says, shaking her head as she peers round the rocks.

'We have to try Bushy,' you remind her. 'What is it that you're always saying? A good explorer never gives up.'

Just then, a terrible noise fills the air. It sounds like a badly out of tune whistle. That can only mean one thing; Stanley the Songful Seahorse must be close at hand. They do so love to sing but are completely tone deaf of course. This gives you an idea . . .

'There might just be a way to use Stanley to help us get past the volcano,' you suggest.

Bushy doesn't look sure and wants to try going round the volcano the long way, avoiding the lava and hoping against all hope that it doesn't blow again.

To agree with Bushy and go the long way round, **turn to page 76.**

Or, to get Stanley to help, **turn to page 49.**

As you creep slowly behind Buster, deep into the heart of the ravine, you start to feel a bitter chill. The snow is coming down thick and fast now, and you begin to wonder whether all this is really worth it to catch sight of a rare Moshling.

'H-h-h-h-h-h-how m-m-much further, B-B-Buster?' you ask, shivering through chattering teeth. 'It's r-r-r-r-reaaally c-c-cold!'

Buster points upwards. 'There, through that gap in the rocks. I'm sure that's the way the Snowtot was heading.'

As Buster moves forward, something catches your eye. A gang of Stunt Penguins are sliding mournfully up and down the snowy hillside. Because their feet don't reach the pedals they are rubbish at riding bikes.

'What's wrong?' you call over.

It turns out that they're lost. They've been doing their best to get back to the Frostipop Glacier, but are now so tired that they can barely even flap.

You have to make a decision quickly. Buster has nearly reached the gap in the rocks and will soon disappear out of sight. Then again, your heart cannot help but melt for the Stunt Penguins. They desperately need help to find their way home and back to a regular supply of pilchard popsicles.

To follow Buster and continue the hunt for the Snowtot, **turn to page 47.**

Or, to stay and help the lost Birdies, **turn to page 54.**

Lenny Lard is keen to assist but can't actually swim! The engine on the sub has given up, so you badly need someone on the outside to fight your corner. What you don't need is someone bobbing about on the waves in a rubber ring, scared that they might tip out at any second.

'This is hopeless,' you call to Bushy, doing your best to plug a leak that has appeared following the latest assault from Cap'n Buck. 'If we don't start moving soon, we're sitting ducks.'

'Can't even do that, sorry. I just can't get her started. There's only so much this old girl can take.'

Suddenly, there comes a sound like a rocket ship being launched. A whhhhiiisssshhhiiinnngg sound like you've never heard before, like some sort of enormous firework. The sea starts to shake and the sub starts a'rockin.

'Oh no!' shouts Bushy, grabbing hold of a rail to steady herself as the sub reels. 'Hold onto your hats – Cap'n Buck must be giving it all he's got!'

Holding on with all your might and wondering if this may be the last thing you ever remember, you notice something and smile.

'Monsterific!'

Bushy looks confused.

'Lenny Lard's come to our rescue,' you explain. 'Why didn't we think of it sooner?'

'Think of what?' Bushy asks, still puzzled.

'I've heard about how high he can get. Lenny's the ultimate diver, you see. He can launch himself out of the water faster than the speed of light! That's what the noise is. I mean, I know he can't swim, but as long as he lands back in his rubber ring he can dive bomb to his heart's content.'

You both peer out of a porthole to see Lenny shooting down towards the water.

'Hold on tight!' you cry, grabbing on to the sub's control panel.

Sssssspppppllllaaaassshhhhhh!!!

The sub is tossed completely out of the water. Luckily, so is Cap'n Buck. The impact snaps him out of his Strangeglove-induced trance. He really can't apologise enough, but you and Bushy can't blame him. He was hypnotised after all, and at least you are finally safe.

'We can finally continue our quest for the Black Pearl', says Bushy. Great, you think . . . but you're going to need a rest before the next adventure!

THE END

You decide that the Penguins will be ok, they're used to the snow after all. Now, you find yourself desperately doing your best to battle through the snowfall to catch up with Buster. He's nearly out of sight.

'Bbbbuuuusteeeerrr!' you yell, wiping snowflakes from your eyes. Luckily, he seems to have stopped moving forward and is now scrabbling up a rock. Driving yourself ahead, you finally reach him.

'Up here . . . quickly!' hisses Buster, pointing down to a gap in the ravine.

You hoist yourself up and join him. 'Look at that,' he whispers. 'Have you ever seen anything more stunning?'

Your eyes scour the foot of the mountains, but it's hard to pick anything out amongst the snow. Suddenly, you spot a movement; a flash moving between the rocks. There's no doubting what it is.

'Amazing,' says Buster. 'Just when you think you've seen everything.'

You both sit and watch quietly for a moment or two. Tomba is shuffling around in the snow beneath you, humming a mournful tune that drifts up to you on the breeze. To see a Moshling as rare as this out in the wild is a wonderful thing, but the sad song reminds you of the Penguins. They looked so lost and hungry, and if you don't go back to help them you worry whether they will ever make it back to Frostipop Glacier.

You tell Buster your concerns.

'I'd love to help,' says Buster. 'Nobody's a bigger fan of a Stunt Penguin than I am, but I really want to add a

Wistful Snowtot to my collection.'

You nod, understandingly.

'Will you be all right on your own if I go?' you ask.

'I'll be fine. The question is, will you be okay missing out on the chance to get near to Tomba?' Buster replies, icicles beginning to form on his moustache as he talks. 'But it's entirely up to you.'

Decisions, decisions, decisions. Why does it always have to be so hard to choose?

To stay with Buster and study Tomba, **turn to page 74.**

Or, to go back and help the lost Penguins, **turn to page 54.**

There's no time to lose, so you rush down to the water's edge to enlist Stanley's help. Clutching your hands over your ears you desperately try to block out the hideous noise, but it's still seeping through. This had better work, you think.

You reach the shallows and splash in through the hot waves. Lava is now creeping down the mountainside and warming up the water. There really is no time to lose.

'Sorry about this,' you say, shuffling forward towards Stanley. He is bobbing about happily, whistling loudly and tunelessly. In a flash, you have scooped him out of the water and are soon making haste down the path back towards the bottom of the volcano. He's clearly surprised by the sudden intrusion into his music, but that certainly doesn't stop him from whistling. Each time he whistles, a barrage of bubbles pours from his mouth, cooling down the ground ahead and allowing you to forge through the lava paths of the island.

'Follow me,' you shout to a stunned Bushy, still sheltering from the volcanic outpour.

'The bubbles are cooling the lava down, so we should be able to get nearer the spot where the exotic worms are.'

'I can see that,' shouts Bushy, blocking her ears. 'But how on earth will we be able to put up with that terrible noise?'

'We'll just have to. It'll be worth it for a worm earring.'

You rush forward, followed by a deafened Bushy and some wincing Musky Huskies. You are managing to carve some sort of path through the lava, but according to Bushy's map there are still miles to go and things are really heating up.

'This is no good!' she shouts. 'We'll never make it. I'm pulling us out while we still have time.'

You know that she's right, but you cannot help but feel upset.

'At least that ear-splittingly noisy seahorse can get us back to the boat. Come on, mission aborted.'

You turn and start to make your way back, hoping that Stanley won't run out of his endless supply of bubbles.

'This lava's coming down thick and fast now,' shouts Bushy. 'We'd better pick up the pace.' She breaks into a run but trips, unfortunately landing lat on her face.

'**Oooowwwww!**' she yelps, then sits up suddenly. 'Well, lookie here.'

You peer down the lava-splattered path and see exactly what she is referring to. A glittery, blinged up Moshling stares straight back at you.

'It's Blingo!' you cry. 'Buster's told me all about him.'

'What on earth's he doing here?' Bushy wonders, scratching her head. 'It's is a long way from the Hipster Hills.'

'He must be looking for a new place to live,' you suggest. Bushy nods and then spots something. 'And look at what he's wearing.'

You had already spotted something glistening on his paw. It's a shiny, shimmering piece of jewellery. It looks almost like a wiggly charm bracelet.

'Wow,' you whisper to yourself, edging forward to get

a closer look.

This is no ordinary bangle – it's alive! These must be the famous exotic worms. The problem is, how are you ever going to get Blingo to part with it?

'As far as I can see, we've got two options here,' you say to Bushy. 'We could try tempting him with a Hip Hop Hibiscus. Flashy Foxes can't resist them. We could try swapping the worm on his bracelet for something similarly sparkly while he's sniffing the plant. He might not even notice, as long as it's shiny.'

Bushy thinks about this, clearly intrigued. 'Go on,' she says. 'You said there were two options.'

'Or, we could try bribing him. Offer up even more bling in return if he'll hand it over.'

To try out the Hip Hop Hibiscus plan, **turn to page 61.**

Or, to bribe him with some bling, **turn to page 69.**

You decide to get help from Octo but are starting to wonder why. To be fair she is trying her best, but simply spraying a fine mist of water at Cap'n Buck really isn't enough stop him attacking you and Bushy.

'This isn't working, sorry!' you call out to Octo, hoping that she has another plan up her tentacle. Luckily, she does. She might not have the fire or water power to take on Cap'n Buck, but she does have a few friends who can add to the numbers. First of all she calls on Myrtle the Diving Turtle, who is enlisted to head down beneath the waves to tackle Cap'n Buck from one side. She then gets hold of Gail Whale and asks her to take him on from the other side. However, it soon becomes apparent that he's just too dangerous to be defeated. He's currently firing Toad Soda out of an underwater canon and those toads really do sting.

Bushy puts on a brave face. 'We gave it our best shot. That's the main thing.'

Kind words, but you can't help but feel terrible. Now you've got Octo, Gail and Myrtle involved so Buck is firing at them too. As Bushy is quick to point out however, the real blame should be laid at Dr. Strangeglove's door. Even though Cap'n Buck is currently causing you some serious issues, you can't help but feel sorry for him. At least he's starting to seem a bit more like his old self, and his eyes no longer look quite so glazed. He appears to be snapping out of the sleepy state he was in. Then, as suddenly as the attack began, a complete change seems to wash over him. He immediately stops attacking the sub and is desperate to explain himself.

'Ar, I be so sorry,' he says sheepishly. 'I knew exactly what I were doing, but there were nothing I could do to stop it. It be that terrible glovey-guts that did put a spell on me. How can I make it up to youse?'

'Don't worry,' you say, relieved to have Buck back to his usual self.

'Actually, there is one thing . . . ' Bushy replies, forgiving her old friend instantly. 'Have you ever heard of the legendary Black Pearl? We could do with a little help tracking one down.'

Octo, Myrtle and Gail, however, are keen to relax after all that excitement with a game of underwater snooker – something you have always wanted to try. You're tempted to leave Bushy to her adventuring and hang out here instead.

You find yourself faced with another dilemma. To continue the quest with Bushy and Cap'n Buck, **turn to page 63.**

Or, to stay and play a very wet game of snooker, **turn to page 73.**

You are heading back to the spot where you last saw the Penguins, and trying your best not to think about the chance you passed up to help Buster with the Snowtot. As you round the corner, you become aware that the valley you left them in is now empty. You stand alone. There is no sign whatsoever of a Penguin, Stunt or otherwise, so you try calling out.

'Peppy?'

No response. Could it be that you gave the adventure up for nothing? Just then, you become aware of something above your head. You can make out a strange movement in the sky. You peer upwards, but all you can see is a flash of feather and flight. You can hardly believe your eyes – it's the Penguins! They seem to be attempting a new kind of high altitude stunt, and there you were worrying about them. You move forward to get a better view of what exactly they're up to, but stop, feeling a crunch underfoot. You look down and see a pile of icy fish bones. No wonder they managed to get their strength back up. They've clearly managed to locate a fresh supply of pilchard popsicles and have munched through enough of them to sink the Cloudy Cloth Clipper.

This leaves you with yet another dilemma. Now that the Penguins seem to be out of danger, you could always leave them to their own devices and try to find your own way home, but it's cold and lonely up here on the mountain and you're not sure you want to wander about any more by yourself.

If you're not afraid of going it alone, **turn to page 59.**

If you want to help the Penguins find a way back to Frostipop Glacier, **turn to page 68.**

'Quick . . . over here!' Bushy shouts. You join her and do everything you can to stop Cap'n Buck from boarding the sub, but nothing seems to be working. He's throwing everything he can at you.

Thud!

'What was that?' you shout, checking for leaks.

'He's attacking us with Slopcorn, now. Not sure how much longer the sub can hold out under this kind of a barrage.'

You peer out through the porthole and flinch as it's splattered with another splodge of Slopcorn.

'Any suggestions gratefully received!' shouts Bushy, as another colossal crash can be heard on the starboard bow.

'I'm all out,' you cry. 'Fighting off food-flinging pirates really isn't my thing.'

Suddenly, a brainwave lightbulb pings on above your head. 'Help!' you shout out.

'Bit busy right now,' responds a confused Bushy.

'No – help's the answer! We should call for help. Presumably this sub can send out a mayday signal?'

Bushy grins and whacks a red button on the control panel. Seconds later, the sub emits a honking distress call to anyone who might be passing. There are two quick responses; one from Octo, who is swimming nearby, and another from Lenny Lard who's paddling about in The Port.

But who to turn to?

To enlist help from Lenny, **turn to page 45.**

Or, to get help from Octo, **turn to page 52.**

You decide that an outing a little closer to home might be the best way to begin adventuring, so are now stowing away on Bushy's latest expedition – a trip to Flutterby Field. Still, you are rapidly discovering that stowing away isn't all it's cracked up to be. You'd been hiding for ages before she'd even set off, and really feel that you might need the toilet soon. Eventually you crack and decide to show yourself. You know that Bushy won't be happy, but you really don't think you can take much more of this. You decide to get the first word in and plead your case.

'Right, before you say anything, I only hid away because I knew you'd turn me down if I asked to come along, and while I know that you might be cross, the important thing to remember here is that . . . '

'Ssssshhhhhh, will you please?' Bushy hisses. 'This is the closest I've ever come to these little beauties. the last thing we want is you scaring them off into his net.'

You're a little confused. Whose net? What's she talking about? You crouch down beside her and peer out into the middle of the field but cannot see anything out of the ordinary.

'What are we looking at?' you ask.

'There. By the Bouncebush.'

You stare a little harder and then spot it: the most colourful flutterby you have ever seen. It's like a tiny rainbow with wings.

'Trouble is,' continues Bushy, 'we're not the only ones who want the little chap.' She points towards the field.

And then you spot him.

About the same distance from the flutterby but on the other side of the field, there stands a familiar figure; net in hand, pith helmet on head, huge moustache billowing in the breeze, there is no mistaking him . . .

'Colonel Catcher,' mumbles Bushy. 'He'll stop at nothing to add that little gem to his collection.'

You know exactly what she's talking about. The Colonel is notoriously famous for his hobby. Obsessed with collecting flutterby species for his Genus of Monstro City whiteboard, Colonel Catcher retired early from his tour of Bendia and can now be found roaming about with his net. To be fair, he is harmless enough, but in Bushy's eyes he is another obstacle; both are after the same rare breed and one of them will have to lose out.

You eye up the situation, feeling like you owe it to Bushy to help her.

'The way I see it, we have two choices here,' you whisper. 'I can either creep round to his side of the field and try to scare the flutterby back towards you, or I can try and reason with him.'

To try your hand at reasoning with the Colonel, **turn to page 66.**

Or, to try scaring the flutterby back towards Bushy, **turn to page 15.**

As you find your way out of the ravine, you decide that this was definitely the best option. Buster is more than capable of taking care of Tomba and the Stunt Penguins seem happy enough. It's time to get back to Bushy. Hopefully, you'll find a way onto her next expedition as soon as she feels up to it. After all, you've already proved yourself to be a worthy addition to any adventure!

You are just about to take the main path back out of the mountains, when you hear a whimper. Looking round, you find it hard to see anything as it is getting dark. You have another look but there really is no one else here, so you press onwards and upwards. You stop suddenly; there it is again – the faintest little whimper! You turn and retrace your steps until you hear the small cry once again. It seems to be coming from behind a bush. Gently, you pull aside a branch and peer within, but immediately jump back at the sight that greets you.

'Hello,' you say. 'Are you all right?'

Whatever is in there looks back at you sadly. The tiniest tear is trickling down a fluffy blue face. You look a little closer.

'Come on,' you say, gently trying to encourage it out of its hiding place. 'What's the matter?'

The creature shuffles timidly forward, revealing itself to be a bright blue Titchy-Tusked Mammoth.

'Hello little one,' you say, gingerly reaching out to ruffle its fur. It seems to like it, although you notice that the Inka-Inka essence it's used to get that shade of blue is still a little damp.

It seems lonely out here in the snow, so you suggest it travels back to Monstro City with you.

As it allows you to lead it away, you spot a smile playing across its mouth, and notice that its tears have dried up. You smile too, knowing that you have done a good turn and found something awesome to take back and show Bushy and Buster.

THE END

Having left Bushy behind to track down a Hip Hop Hibiscus plant, you set about returning Stanley. Your eardrums are almost ready to burst and you manage to get him back to the sea just in time.

'Thanks Stanley!' you shout, as you drop him into the waves. 'You've been a great help.'

You dash back to find Bushy crouching down behind a tree and peering out at the plant.

'Anything yet?' you ask breathlessly, sliding in beside her to watch and hoping that Blingo takes the bait.

'You sure this will work?' she murmurs. 'I've been here a long time and nothing's happened so far.'

'Trust me. According to Buster, he can't resist that crazy Hibiscus scent.'

Sure enough, as soon as the aroma of the Hibiscus wafts out into the wind, Blingo steps out, nose twitching.

'Look at him,' you say. 'He's drawn to it like a Baby Tumteedum to boiled cabbage. Just like I said he would be.'

You both watch for a moment or two, then Bushy snaps into action.

'Keep a look out for me – I'm going in!'

Before Blingo even has time to notice, she's snaffled the exotic worm from his wrist and replaced it with another sparkly charm.

'Mission accomplished!' she says, creeping back. 'There's so much bling on his wrist, I'm surprised he can lift his arm up to touch the Hibiscus.'

You nod in agreement. Blingo doesn't seem to have noticed the difference at all.

'Time to head back to Monstro City,' says Bushy. 'We need to get these valuables back to the Bizarre Bazaar. My customers will be wondering where I've got to!'

THE END

You and Bushy are heading back down to the seabed. Luckily, Cap'n Buck insisted on mending the engine to try and repay you both for his bad behaviour. Bushy kept telling him that she didn't blame him for a second, but he felt so awful and really was keen to join in the expedition.

'Slow down a little. Now, turn twenty-seven degrees left. That's it, easy does it.'

Cap'n Buck is working the controls, while Bushy is studying her map and shouting out instructions.

'Right, now stop. We should be just over the Black Pearl beds,' says Bushy.

Cap'n Buck screeches the sub to a halt. You bob about for a bit, keeping your eyes peeled, until Bushy suddenly points.

'There!'

You all stare through the gloom of the murky water. In the midst of a bed of rocks and weed shimmers a moon-like glow. Your eyes cannot help but be drawn to the light. It has a dark beauty to it.

'Thar it be,' says Cap'n Buck.

'The mystical Black Pearl,' whispers Bushy. 'I never thought I'd see the day.'

'I hate to spoil the party, but it's not going to be as easy as just picking it up,' you point out. 'Look.'

Bushy and Cap'n Buck immediately pick up on the problem: a Valley Mermaid is keeping guard.

'Barnacles!' exclaims Bushy. 'No offence intended,' she says to Cap'n Buck. 'So close, yet so far.'

Once again, you are able to come to the rescue.

'Hang on a Moshi moment!' you shout. 'I've got it.

Stick the kettle on!'

Immediately, Bushy's eyes light up.

'Of course . . . cappuccinos all round!'

With a smile, you mix up some hot frothy coffee and waft the smell in Cali the Valley Mermaid's direction. She is, like, totally drawn to you and swims over to catch up on all the latest gossip from Monstro City.

Bushy swipes the Black Pearl and gives you a wink. You grin back, happy to have helped.

THE END

As you do your best to steer yourself towards Bushy and the Huskies, you thank your lucky stars for the blanket. Even with it flapping about above your head, you are still travelling at quite a speed, and it's not exactly easy to steer. Luckily, a gust of wind picks you up and turns you in the right direction.

Eventually however, after a good deal of to-ing and a little bit of fro-ing, you find yourself directly above Bushy and the Huskies. With a sharp tug to the left and a yank to the right, you try to land neatly in front of them. If only; all you actually manage to do is plummet into the midst of the pack and send Bushy flying.

'Potty Pipsqueaks!' she shouts, as she goes hurtling into a huddle of Huskies, sending them scampering.

Then you spot it. It has fallen from her bag and is lying glistening in the dust: the magnificent 18 Carat Shiny Parrot. It almost takes your breath away with its beauty.

'See you found it then?' you say to Bushy, as she stumbles to her feet and dusts herself down. 'Definitely worth the trip then?'

'You can say that again. Just look at the gloopendous little beauty.'

She picks up the Parrot and cradles it like a baby. You can see now why she does what she does – the danger is always worth it for a find like this.

'Shame you couldn't join us,' Bushy says, sensing your disappointment. 'We had quite an adventure getting it.'

'Don't worry,' you say, smiling. 'I've had one or two adventures myself!'

THE END

You decide to try and reason with the Colonel. Well, how hard can it be? After all, he's always seemed like a nice enough chap. You creep out from your hiding place.

'Be careful,' whispers Bushy, as you sidle across the field, keeping your head down. 'Remember, if you scare that flutterby off we may never get a chance like this again. Sightings are virtually unheard of.'

You ignore her. You have enough to think about, like planning your strategy on how to approach the Colonel. This calls for tact and diplomacy. Charm and plenty of smiles is definitely the key here.

Just as you get close to him, you see that he's poised and ready to pounce. With his moustache bristling and a net in one hand, he creeps closer and closer towards the flutterby. You edge forward and cough discretely. He turns and looks at you in surprise. Just as you're about to explain what you are doing there, he flings himself forward and the equally surprised flutterby suddenly finds itself under the netting. You're too late, and now Bushy really will be cross at losing this prized treasure.

The Colonel watches the flutterby flap about in his net for a second or two, before turning to look at you. Remembering your plan, you turn on the charm and try to keep smiling as you explain what you want. You describe how for years Bushy had been searching desperately for the flutterby, and that while you would completely understand if he were to say no, perhaps there might be some way he could let you have it to take back to her.

The Colonel thinks about your proposition for a

while, then nods.

'What a jolly good chum of Bushy's you must be,' he says. 'I am sure we can come to some arrangement.'

He explains that his collection is very special to him and that he is worried about intruders. If you could help him out with some extra security, he might be persuaded to hand the creature over.

You think back to what Bushy has in her shop . . .

'How about we do a swap?' you say. 'Two rolls of Roaring Mouth Wallpaper to scare off any unwanted visitors and an Eye Plant to keep an eye on things while you're out catching flutterbies.'

The Colonel nods again, satisfied.

A few minutes later, you find yourself walking back to Bushy with the flutterby flapping about in a jar. She had better be pleased with you! While Bushy gets her flutterby, you get to spend the next few days decorating the Colonel's dusty old shed . . .

THE END

You watch intently as the Penguins attempt ever more dangerous stunts. This is no good at all. It will achieve nothing, though you have to admit it's impressive. You are just about to start getting cross with them when Peppy swings down, and before you know it you are caught up in the stunt. As Peppy performs a high loop the loop, you find yourself sailing through the air. Before you've had time to even catch your breath, you are upside down.

'Whhhhaaaagghhhh!' you yell, as dizziness starts to take over.

'Wwwwweeeee!' you cry out, in the hope that somehow you'll end up back on your feet. However, as you loop around once more, you spot something.

'Hang on a second, Peppy. Do that again,' you call.

This time you are able to make certain.

'Oh, yes. You know what that is, don't you?' you cry, pointing at a far off spot in the distance. 'It's Frostipop Glacier. I'm sure of it.'

The Penguins look where you are pointing and smiles break out across their beaks; you have shown them the way home!

Now there's just the small matter of getting back to Monstro City yourself, but you can deal with that now you've helped the very grateful Penguins find their way back home. You really have saved the day.

THE END

You realise quite quickly that your decision to try and bribe Blingo may not have been the best one. Bushy is trying to offer him everything she has, but he's just not taking it.

'There must be something we can give him that he'll fancy more than the worm on his wrist?' says Bushy. She tries holding out a shiny, chunky neck chain, but soon turns away in frustration after he shakes his head, disinterested.

'Solastseason,' he mutters.

'How about we offer to take him back to Monstro City to do some shopping?' you suggest.

Blingo's eyes light up at this, sparkling like the medallion around his neck.

'TakemetoMarketplace? Goodthreadsthere.'

It takes you a minute to work out what he's saying, but when you do, inspiration strikes you.

'Maybe we're going about this the wrong way,' you say, turning to Bushy. 'Blingo enjoys a bit of fashion, right? But he's already the hippest Moshling in town. What we need to give him is something, or someone, totally unfashionable to zing up a bit. You know, like a makeover . . .'

'Oh no,' she says, immediately catching your drift. 'You can't be serious.'

'Do you want that exotic worm or not?' you ask, noticing that Blingo is smiling excitedly at the prospect of restyling Bushy's image.

Exactly one hour later, Bushy is standing before you looking super funky, if not super happy. Her hair is backcombed into the biggest quiff you've ever laid eyes on and Blingo has stuck so many sequins onto her white coat that she glitters like a disco ball. Still, at least she has the exotic worm in her possession, even if Blingo is insisting she wears it balanced across the top of her specs. Job done! Though admittedly it may take a while for her to forgive you . . .

THE END

Having checked that the flutterby is still bumbling around the Bouncebush, you venture over towards Lila Tweet and Pete Slurp's picnic. They are currently chomping through Lila's mother's famous Quenut Butter Sandwiches, and Lila is singing another tune. You stop and listen for a second. Lila really is a fabulous singer – not that Pete seems particularly interested. Always keen on collecting rare slugs, he's just spotted a fat and juicy specimen slithering its way across the field and is doing his best to catch it without Lila noticing. As she reaches a particularly high note, Pete pounces and manages to trap the slippery customer under an empty Quenut Butter jar.

Politely, but impatiently, you wait for Lila to finish her tune. You are desperate to get to the flutterby before it flaps away. Finally, she reaches the end and you are able to explain your predicament to them both. You ask if Lila would mind coming across and singing to the flutterby, in the hope that her gentle melodies will entice it over to Bushy and her waiting net. Lila is flattered; she had always known she was the best singer in school, but to discover that her voice might be good enough to hypnotise a flutterby is quite a compliment! She agrees at once.

You lead Lila over to the hedge at the edge of the field and you both peer over. The flutterby is just out of reach.

You signal to Bushy to stand by with the net, and then turn to Lila and nod. It's time to unleash her gift of song on the unsuspecting flutterby . . .

She coughs a little and then lets rip. As the haunting

melody floats out into the breeze, the flutterby seems to pause mid-flight, before turning around and heading towards you and Lila.

'Keep singing,' you whisper, as you start to walk towards Bushy. 'It's following.'

Gently, you lead it across to where Bushy is waiting and seconds later the flutterby finds itself in her net. Bushy is over the moon! To celebrate, Lila asks you both to join the picnic. As you munch on a sandwich and watch the flutterby flap about cheerfully in the net, Lila breaks into another song. Happy days!

THE END

You decide to take on Octo, Gail Whale and Myrtle at underwater snooker, only you're finding it's not as easy as you first thought. Not only do you have to keep heading for the surface, taking a huge gulp of air in and then swimming down really quickly to take your shot, but the snooker balls also keep floating off with the current.

Despite this, you discover that you're actually pretty awesome at it. You manage to knock Myrtle the Diving Turtle out in the first round. She might be brilliant at hunting, but she's no match for your potting skills. She can hardly believe it when you sink the final black ball, (and you literally do sink it.) At the end of the match, everyone has to spend a lot of time looking for it on the seabed.

Next up in the semi-final is Gail Whale. You make short work of her, leaving only Octo to beat for the trophy. Much to everyone's excitement in Monstro City, Gail even broadcasts the match live on Moshi TV. It's a close run thing for a few frames but then you pull out your trump card; a three ball pot in one move! And that's even more difficult than it sounds, considering you had to bounce the cue ball off a crab in order to achieve it. Still, Octo is gracious in defeat. To much clapping of fins and pincers, you are crowned underwater snooker champ of the year!

THE END

Tomba is just too cool to resist. You watch as Buster creeps forward quietly, before beckoning you to come and join him. You shuffle ahead, really very pleased that you decided to stay and observe this rare Snowtot. It truly is a magnificent specimen and it seems more concerned with trying to get its droopy beanie to stay on its head than worrying about the pair of you creeping up behind it. Buster gestures to you to go round the other side, so you set off on a pincer movement.

You've never seen a Snowtot before and cannot wait to tell everyone back in Monstro City. However, just as you shuffle forward it looks up and notices you. Both you and Buster hold your breath; has it all been for nothing? If it makes a run for it, you may never get a chance to record the moment. It will be gone forever, back into the ice and you will have no proof of ever having seen it. You think about grabbing your camera and snapping away, but decide against it. If you're the one responsible for scaring it off, Buster will never speak to you again.

Suddenly, it catches you both by surprise by scooting an ice puck forward and then chasing behind it, brushing the ice in front of the puck with a stick. Very strange behaviour indeed!

'Oh, right. I get it,' smiles Buster. You look confused for a second.

'They love curling,' Buster explains. 'If we offer to play with it, it should cheer up in no time.'

Soon enough, you see it smiling faintly as you set up a

ame; a curling competition that sees Tomba beating both
ou and Buster very easily indeed. Cool!

THE END

You and Bushy are wending your way round the volcano, keeping one eye nervously on it. She really could blow any minute. You can tell Bushy's quite concerned by the speed she's driving the Musky Huskies onwards. Then suddenly she relaxes.

'We should be okay here, even if there is an eruption,' she says, slowing down gently.

You stop to catch your breath and look round.

'Where are we?' you ask, unable to spot anything even vaguely recognisable.

'Skip 'n' jump Creek, by my calculations,' Bushy explains. 'I brought us this way because there's been occasional sightings of exotic worms round here. I'm not giving up on the mission just because of a bit of hot lava.'

'Didn't think you would,' you say smiling.

You feel a rumble under your feet. For a brief second you panic thinking it's the volcano, until you manage to spot where it's coming from. An old Hickopotumus is fast asleep up ahead and snoring so loudly that the Huskies start backing away nervously.

'Great . . . ' says Bushy, 'now what? I'll never get them to go round. Not with that racket blasting out. We'll either have to shift him or go back.'

'But then we'll never find an exotic worm,' you point out. Besides, you think you may have a solution or two.

'There are only a couple of ways to wake a Snoring Hickopotumus, as far as I can remember. How about some extremely loud banjo playing? That's been known to work!'

'Or?' asks Bushy hopefully. 'I'm not exactly known

or my musical skills, and besides, where would we find a anjo out here?'

'Luckily, I just so happen to have one with me,' you humble shyly. 'I like to play a little.'

'What's the other way?' asks Bushy as you reach into jour backpack. You whip out the banjo and pluck, trying to ignore Bushy as she winces at your first note.

'We organise a barn dance. They can't resist them.'

To try the banjo playing idea, **turn to page 9.**

Or, to give the barn dance plan a whirl, **turn to page 17.**

You have stowed away on the back of Bushy's mountai[n] wagon in order to join her on an epic journey to the depth[s] of the Gombala Gombala jungle, as she seeks out th[e] legendary 18 Carat Shiny Parrot. It was far from easy bu[t] you managed to creep in and curl up into a ball.

'One, two, three . . . ' you count to yourself. 'Surprise!'

You leap out from your hiding place, but sadly it's not into an amazing Bushy Fandango exploration. You clumsily miss your footing as you jump and end up getting flung completely out of the wagon, landing flat on your face in the middle of the jungle.

'Hey, Bushy!' you shout.

But she doesn't hear a thing. The Musky Huskies are baying excitedly and there's no way she'd have noticed your spectacular plunge. You clamber up, dust yourself off, and wonder what to do next.

To try and chase after Bushy and hope that you'll catch up with her if the Huskies slow down, **turn to page 7.**

Or, to try and find a shortcut to head them off further up the valley, **turn to page 11.**